BAD ACTOR

Keith Edward Vaughn

BLONDIE ST

Bad Actor by Keith Edward Vaughn

Published by Blondie Street Publishing
Chattanooga, TN

www.keithedwardvaughn.com

Cover by Melissa McMurtrie

Formatting by Melissa McMurtrie

ISBN: 979-8-9865319-2-2 (paperback)

ISBN: 979-8-9865319-3-9 (ebook)

Library of Congress Control Number: 2025911868

Printed in the U.S.A.

First Edition

Praise for THE LONELIEST PLACES

"The Loneliest Places isn't just a terrific debut, it's authentic L.A. noir—the city breathing and bleeding right alongside the troubled souls slinking through its pages. Continuing in the tradition of Nathanael West and James M. Cain, Keith Edward Vaughn reminds us that the brighter the sunlight, the darker the shadows."

— Joseph Schneider, critically acclaimed author of the Detective Tully Jarsdel mysteries

"★★★★ A mesmerizing exploration of one man's journey through the underworld of a city and his own inner demons."

— Literary Titan

"Crisp, wry, fleet-moving prose... [A] promising series starter."

— BookLife

"A gritty, assured mystery debut, right up to its satisfying final notes."

— Kirkus Reviews

"A smart, sharp, entertaining, and exhilarating debut that tells a darkly humorous noir story about the seedy underbelly of glamorous modern-day Los Angeles."

— IndieReader

"An atmospheric, suspenseful and wistful work of L.A. noir. Recommended for fans of Lisa Gray and Michael Connelly."

— BestThrillers.com

"Similar to the work of James Ellroy... The Loneliest Places is a modern slice of hardboiled noir set in a version of L.A. that is both familiarly terrible and unexpectedly uplifting."

— Independent Book Review

Also by KEITH EDWARD VAUGHN

The Loneliest Places

for Mary Payne